Alex
Remembers

by HELEN V. GRIFFITH
pictures by DONALD CARRICK

Greenwillow Books, New York

Library of Congress Cataloging in Publication Data
Griffith, Helen V.   Alex remembers.
Summary: A dog and cat are restless and troubled in
the autumn moonlight as primordial fears stir in them,
but their young owner is there to comfort them.
[1. Animals—Fiction.   2. Moon—Fiction]
I. Carrick, Donald, ill.   II. Title.
PZ7.G8823Am 1983   [E]   82-11913
ISBN 0-688-01800-9
ISBN 0-688-01801-7 (lib. bdg.)

FOR WHIPPET

Alex and the cat were restless.
"Please sit still," said Robbie.
But they couldn't.

They paced the floor and made wild noises
in their throats.
"Please stop that," said Robbie.
But they couldn't.
"Maybe you need some exercise," said Robbie.
He opened the door and sent them outside.

Alex and the cat sat on the porch and
watched the moon rise round and orange.

They smelled leaf smoke.
They heard geese calling from the dark sky.

Alex threw back his head and howled.
"That's funny," he said. "I rarely howl."
The cat glanced at him and back at
the moon. "You're remembering," he said.
"Remembering what?" asked Alex.
"Things," said the cat.
Alex pointed his nose toward the sky
and howled again.
"It's something about the moon," he said.

"I know," said the cat. He gazed into the darkness through half-closed eyes. "We remember sometimes— in the fall, mostly—when the moon looks like that."

"What do we remember?" asked Alex.
"Wait," said the cat.

A mist was rising from the field
beyond the fence.

There were sounds in the mist—chomps and
crunches and squishes and thumps.

Something flapped up out of the mist
and flew across the moon.

"Can lizards fly?" asked Alex.

The cat's tail began to switch from side to side.
He snarled.

"What is it?" whispered Alex.
"Look," growled the cat.

Alex looked. He saw shadows in the mist.
"They look like ferns," said Alex. "But are they?"

Other shadows moved among the fern shadows.
"They look like animals," said Alex. "But are they?"
He moved closer to the cat.

A long snaky neck rose above the mist and swayed toward them. The cat flattened his ears and hissed.

"Oh my," said Alex. Something ROARED!
The snaky neck swayed back into the mist.

Something SCREECHED!
The fern shadows waved wildly.
Something SCREAMED!
Alex jumped to his feet.
"Are they fighting?" he asked. "Could they hurt us? Are they coming? Should we run?"
"Calm down," said the cat.

Something behind them SLAMMED!
The cat shrieked and leaped
from the porch.
 Alex shut his eyes.
"Help," he whispered.
"What's wrong with the cat?"
 Robbie asked.

He sat down with his arm around Alex.
"You're cold," he said.

Alex wanted to say, "We've been remembering."
But he just leaned against Robbie and shivered.

The cat came back.
He sat close to Robbie and purred.

"Look at the moon," Robbie said.
"I've never seen it so big and orange."

Is he remembering? Alex wondered, and
he looked at Robbie's face.
But Robbie was only looking at the moon.